It's time for action.
COWS IN ACTION!

Genius cow Professor McMoo and his
trusty sidekicks, Pat and Bo, are star
agents of the C.I.A. – short for
COWS IN ACTION!
They travel through time, fighting evil
bulls from the future and keeping
history on the right track . . .

Find out more at
www.cowsinaction.com

Read all the adventures of
McMoo, Pat and Bo:

THE TER-MOO-NATORS

Coming soon!

THE ROMAN MOO-STERY

also by Steve Cole:

ASTROSAURS

Riddle of the Raptors
The Hatching Horror
The Seas of Doom
The Mind-Swap Menace
The Skies of Fear
The Space Ghosts
Day of the Dino-Droids
The Terror-Bird Trap
The Planet of Peril
Teeth of the T. rex
(specially published for WBD)

Coming soon!
The Star Pirates
The Claws of Christmas

THE MOO-MY'S CURSE

Steve Cole

Illustrated by Woody Fox

RED FOX

THE MOO-MY'S CURSE
A RED FOX BOOK 978 1 862 30190 0

First published in Great Britain by Red Fox,
an imprint of Random House Children's Books

This edition published 2007

3 5 7 9 10 8 6 4 2

Set in Bembo Schoolbook by
Falcon Oast Graphic Art Ltd.

Red Fox Books are published by Random House Children's Books,
61–63 Uxbridge Road, London W5 5SA

www.**kids**at**randomhouse**.co.uk

Addresses for companies within
The Random House Group Limited can be found at:
www.randomhouse.co.uk/offices.htm

THE RANDOM HOUSE GROUP Limited Reg. No. 954009

A CIP catalogue record for this book is available from the British Library.

Printed in the UK by CPI Bookmarque, Croydon, CR0 4TD

For Nathan and Cassie Dallaire

★ THE C.I.A. FILES ★

Cows from the present –
Fighting in the past to protect the future . . .

In the year 2550, after thousands of years of being eaten and milked, cows finally live as equals with humans in their own country of Luckyburger. But a group of evil war-loving bulls – the Fed-up Bull Institute – is not satisfied.

Using time machines and deadly ter-moo-nator agents, the F.B.I. is trying to change Earth's history. These bulls plan to enslave all humans and put savage cows in charge of the planet. Their actions threaten to plunge all cowkind into cruel and cowardly chaos . . .

The C.I.A. was set up to stop them.

However, the best agents come not from the present – but from the past. From a time in the early 21st century, when the first clever cows began to appear. A time when a brainy bull named Angus McMoo invented the first time machine, little realizing he would soon become the F.B.I.'s number one enemy . . .

COWS OF COURAGE — TOP SECRET FILES

PROFESSOR ANGUS MCMOO

Security rating: Bravo Moo Zero

Stand-out features: Large white squares on coat, outstanding horns

Character: Scatterbrained, inventive, plucky and keen

Likes: Hot tea, history books, gadgets

Hates: Injustice, suffering, poor-quality tea bags

Ambition: To invent the electric sundial

LITTLE BO VINE

Security rating: For your cow pies only

Stand-out features: Luminous udder (colour varies)

Character: Tough, cheeky, ready-for-anything rebel

Likes: Fashion, chewing gum, self-defence classes

Hates: Bessie Barmer: the farmer's wife

Ambition: To run her own martial arts club for farmyard animals

PAT VINE

Security rating: Licence to fill (stomach with grass)

Stand-out features: Zigzags on coat

Character: Brave, loyal and practical

Likes: Solving problems, anything Professor McMoo does

Hates: Flies not easily swished by his tail

Ambition: To find a five-leaf clover — and to survive his dangerous missions!

Prof. McMoo's TIMELINE OF NOTABLE HISTORICAL EVENTS

13.7 billion years BC
BIG BANG - UNIVERSE BEGINS
(and first tea atoms created)

4.6 billion years BC
PLANET EARTH FORMS
(good job too)

23 million years BC
FIRST COWS APPEAR

(23 million is my lucky number!)

1700 BC
SHEN NUNG MAKES FIRST CUP OF TEA
(what a hero!)

7000 BC
FIRST CATTLE KEPT ON FARMS
(Not a great year for cows)

2550 BC
GREAT PYRAMID BUILT AT GIZA
(by an Egyptian geezer)

1901 AD
QUEEN VICTORIA DIES
(she was no a-moo-sed)

31 BC ROMAN EMPIRE FOUNDED

(Roam-Moo empire founded by a cow but no one remembers that)

1509 AD HENRY VIII COMES TO THE THRONE

(and probably squashes it)

1066 AD BATTLE OF HASTINGS

(but what about the Cattle of Hastings??)

1620 AD ENGLISH PILGRIMS SETTLE IN AMERICA

(bringing with them the first cows to moo in an American accent)

1939 AD WORLD WAR TWO BEGINS

or World War Moo as it is known to cows)

2007 AD I INVENT A TIME MACHINE!!!

2500 AD COW NATION OF LUCKYBURGER FOUNDED

(HOORAY!)

(about time!)

1903 AD FIRST TEABAGS INVENTED

2550 AD COWS IN ACTION RECRUIT PROFESSOR McMOO, PAT AND BO

(and now the fun REALLY starts...)

THE MOO-MY'S CURSE

Chapter One

A MOO MISSION

Pat Vine was talking to a rubbish skip. "Hurry up, Professor!" the young bullock hissed, checking the field was still deserted. "We could be spotted at any moment!"

"Yeah, get *moo*-ving, Prof!" added his older sister, a cow called Little Bo Vine.

A pair of hooves emerged from the skip. "Hang on!" came a muffled voice. "I'm sure that cable I need is in here somewhere . . ."

Both the voice and the hooves belonged to Professor Angus McMoo – a brilliantly brainy bull. Like Pat and Bo, he belonged to a rare breed of clever cattle called the Emmsy Squares. The

3

skip, on the other hand, belonged to a brilliant scientist who lived in the house next door. He chucked away all sorts of hi-tech stuff that came in very handy for the amazing project Professor McMoo was working on . . .

Pat looked about nervously. "If Bessie Barmer finds we've got out of our field again, she'll blow her top at us!"

"If she does, I'll blow my *bottom* at her!" Little Bo declared. She was a feisty cow, who liked fights and dyeing her

udder outrageous colours. Today she had dyed it bright blue, and she was thinking about adding pink polka dots.

Like McMoo, Pat and Bo lived on a quiet organic farm. Old Farmer Barmer was nice enough, but his wife, Bessie, was horrid. She hated all the animals and couldn't wait to send them off to the butcher's. Which was why Professor McMoo had started raiding the scientist's rubbish for bits of techno-junk in the first place. Using only his incredible mind, a billion bits and pieces and a lifelong love of history, he had designed and built a super-special, super-secret invention that could take them away from the farm for ever . . .

He had turned his cow shed into a time machine!

"Got it!" cried McMoo. His big brown head popped up from the skip, eyes agleam and with a thick red wire tangled around his horns. "This special cable should allow us to travel faster than ever."

Pat gulped. "Better start travelling right now – here comes Bessie Barmer!"

"Oi! You cows!" The farmer's wife came charging towards them. Bessie was as big as a barn door, with a face like a bulldog licking cold porridge off a thistle. "I've warned you before about going through the bins!"

Little Bo raised her hooves. "Shall I sort her out with a *kung-moo* chop, Professor?"

"If you try that, she'll turn you *into* a chop!" said Pat, rolling his eyes. "Fighting isn't the answer to everything, you know."

"It *is*," said Bo.

Pat scowled. "Oh yeah? What's two plus two, then?"

"Fighting," said Bo, and cuffed him round the horn.

6

"Wanna ask me what's three plus three?"

"That's enough, you two," said Professor McMoo. "And, Bo, you will *not* chop Bessie. She thinks we are ordinary, stupid cows. We must never let her find out our incredible secret."

Pat looked at the professor. "Which secret?" he asked. "That we are special

time agents sworn to stop evil bulls from the future messing up Earth's history? Or that we are the only cows in the world able to peel a banana with our hooves?"

McMoo gave him a look. "The first one, Pat. Come on, let's clear off back to the Time Shed!" With that, he charged off towards the rickety shed in the next-field-but-one, Little Bo and Pat close behind him.

"That's right, hoof it, you beefy beggars!" raged Barmer, shaking her huge fist. "If I catch you in those bins again, I'll have you stuffed! My famous ancestor Sheba Um-Barmer was a champion stuffer! She ran the top mummy-making shop in Ancient Egypt!"

"*Herd* it all before," said McMoo, slowing down to a trot.

"Bessie's always going on about her world-famous ancestors, isn't she?" Pat said.

"I reckon they were all big fat losers," Little Bo put in. "I bet I could take on any of them, blindfolded in a sack with three hooves tied behind my back and a peg on my udder."

"I'd like to see you try," said Pat. Then he thought again, and shuddered. "Actually, no I wouldn't!"

Soon they reached the shed. As ever it seemed empty aside from a few piles of hay. But then Professor McMoo kicked away a small haystack to reveal a large bronze lever and yanked on it hard.

Pat braced himself and sure enough the usual loud, rattling, clanking sound started up. The wooden walls swung round to reveal curious controls and cables and flashing lights on the other side. A large computer screen swung down from the rafters, and a huge bank of controls in the shape of a horseshoe slid up from the ground to fill the middle of the shed. Hidden panels creaked into view on every wall, covered in dials and switches and levers. There was even a large wardrobe that popped up from the ground, stuffed full of clothes from all times and places. In a

matter of moments, the ordinary cow shed had become an extraordinary control room (with a fitting room on the side), throbbing with incredible energy.

While the professor dashed about from panel to panel checking his precious controls, Pat pulled out a kettle from a pile of straw. Any moment now, Professor McMoo would ask for a nice cup of tea – "A hot milky drink helps a bull to think" was his motto. But as Pat went to open a box of tea bags, an alarm went off and all the lights started flashing red. Pat jumped about a mile in the air.

"What's going on, Professor?" he cried. "I wasn't trying to steal them!"

"It's not you," said McMoo, hurrying over to the big screen hanging over the horseshoe. "It means we've got a *moo's-flash*."

Bo looked at him blankly. "A what?"

"Like a newsflash, but with added cows," explained the professor, flicking some switches to stop the alarm. Then he perched some glasses on his nose. "It's the C.I.A. hotline!"

"Cool!" cried Little Bo, joining him eagerly in front of the screen. "They must have a new mission for us!"

C.I.A. was short for Cows in Action, a crack team of time-travelling cow commandos who had recruited Professor McMoo and his friends. They came from the twenty-sixth century, an age where clever cows were commonplace, and they were always on their guard against the F.B.I. – the Fed-up Bull Institute.

McMoo turned on the screen and a hefty black bull with large curly horns appeared on the

screen. He was wearing a dark suit and a blue sash around his chest. "Hey, Professor," said the tough-looking bull. "This is Director Yak of the C.I.A. How's it going?"

"All right." McMoo waved his red cable around. "I'm just rewiring the time-drift controls to maximize the Time Shed's lateral thrust, resulting in a four-point-three-seven per cent increase in year acceleration."

Yak's eyes glazed over. "Right."

"We're all fine, Director," called Pat as he made the tea. "What's the news?"

"Yeah, come on, Yak," said Bo, blowing a gum bubble. "Spill!"

"The F.B.I. is up to something again," said Yak grimly. "According to top-secret reports, they have been sending time machines to Ancient Egypt in the year 1250 BC."

"1250 BC?" echoed McMoo in horror. "But that's a *rubbish* year! Boring, boring, boring. Now, if they'd only gone to 2800 BC they would have seen the first ever pyramid being built and—"

"Er, Professor," hissed Pat. "Shouldn't we hear what Yak has to say?"

"Goody-goody," said Bo.

"I am not!" Pat protested.

"Quiet, you two," said McMoo

sternly. "I'm trying to hear what Yak has to say!"

Yak sighed. "1250 BC must be a weak point in time – a place where history is extra-easy to change. We believe there are other F.B.I. agents already at work in Egypt at that time – and a ter-moo-nator was sent there very recently . . ."

Pat gulped. The thought of a ter-moo-nator gave him butterflies in all four parts of his stomach. Half robot, half bull and all nasty, ter-moo-nators were the F.B.I.'s meanest, toughest agents with super-sneaky computer brains.

Yak went on. "This is your mission – to stop those barking bulls' plans, whatever they are, and keep history on the right track."

Pat felt a shiver of nervous excitement as he poured the professor's tea into a big bucket. It looked like another mind-boggling adventure was coming their way!

"Do you know where the F.B.I. time

machine has landed?" asked Professor McMoo.

The burly bull nodded. "In the Valley of the Kings, in the tomb of Tutankhamen."

"Tooting Car Horn?" echoed Bo blankly.

"Toot-an-car-*moon*," the professor corrected her, saying the word how it sounded. "He was a famous king of Egypt, the twelfth pharaoh of the eighteenth dynasty who ruled during the—"

"Yes, well," Yak interrupted. "I'm beaming over the time-place data now." Lights flickered on the horseshoe of controls. "Be careful, team – and good luck."

The big bull's picture faded from the screen.

Pat passed McMoo his bucket of tea. "Wow, Professor! Ancient Egypt!" he said excitedly. A thought struck him.

"Maybe we'll run into Bessie Barmer's old relative after all!"

"Ugh!" groaned Bo. "Surely we can't be that unlucky."

"Unlucky?" McMoo gulped down the entire bucket of tea and smacked his lips. "We're the luckiest cows in the world!" He rushed around the Time Shed flicking switches and fussing over read-outs. "Just think, humans only discovered the tomb of Tutankhamen in 1922. But we're going back in time to when it was nearly new!" He mooed loudly, coiled his tail around the red take-off lever and smiled at Pat and Bo. "Next stop, Ancient Egypt. It's time for *action*!"

Chapter Two

TERROR IN THE TOMB

In a blaze of purple light, the Time Shed
rattled back into reality. It landed inside
a large cold room made of huge stone
blocks.

"We've arrived!" cried Professor
McMoo. "September 3rd, 1250 BC. Just
coming up to three o'clock in the
morning."

"Cool," said Bo. "I love staying up
late!"

"And if I'm right, there should be quite
a sight outside . . ." Professor McMoo
quickly struggled into some white
Egyptian robes he'd found in the Time
Shed's costume cupboard. Outfits for

18

every single century had been carefully chosen by C.I.A. experts to help the special agents to fit in to any time in history – although McMoo hoped they wouldn't wind up in the Stone Age any time soon. The tiger-skin pants did not look comfy at all. "Come on, you two, get dressed!" he called. "I can't *wait* to get exploring!"

"Me neither," said Pat. "I just hope we don't run straight into a ter-moo-nator."

"Not unless we're driving a tank, anyway," said Little Bo, squeezing into a white linen dress. "Do they have tanks in this time, Professor?"

He shook his head. "Not for another three thousand years or so, I'm afraid."

"I expect the tank would come off worse, in any case," said Pat, putting on a sort of white kilt that young Egyptians used to wear.

"Don't forget your ringblenders, you two," McMoo reminded them, pushing a large silver ring through his nose. Ringblenders were very useful C.I.A. inventions. They projected an optical illusion, so that any cow wearing one could blend in perfectly with human beings. They also translated cow-speak into any language in any time. But only human beings could be fooled by ringblenders. Another cow would recognize their true "moo" nature at once – including the ter-moo-nator . . .

Pat pushed his own ringblender into place and looked at himself in a special mirror that showed his reflection the way humans would see it. He looked like a skinny young boy, his head shaved except for a thick black plait hanging from the side.

Bo smirked. "Nice

hair, Pat. If I pull on it, will your head fall off?"

"Don't worry, Pat, it's the fashion for boys," said the professor, joining them. His reflection showed a noble-

looking man with short dark hair. He wore his blue C.I.A. sash around his neck like a fancy collar.

"Anyway, Bo, you can't talk," said

Pat, pointing to her reflection. It showed a girl with braids and curls in her long black hair and loads of black make-up around her eyes. "You look like a panda in a wig!"

"I do not, I look cool!" Bo retorted. "Don't I, Professor?"

McMoo shrugged. "Very probably – now *come on!*"

"Shouldn't we call up the Tutankhamen file on the computer before we go outside?" asked Pat.

McMoo sighed loudly, itching to be off. But he knew Pat was right, and typed in the name, and words streamed onto the big screen.

++Tutankhamen. ++Ruled over Egypt 1334–1323 BC, from the age of nine. ++His mother-in-law was Nefertiti, famous and beautiful Queen of Egypt. ++Wore make-up and solid gold sandals. Nice! ++Died aged twenty, most likely from a manky leg, which went mouldy after he broke it. ++Replaced by his chief advisor, Ay.

"Ay-aye," Bo joked. "Well, that was really interesting, Professor. I almost feel like I knew him."

"You wouldn't want to know him now," McMoo assured her. "He's been pickled and preserved for years and years, all wrapped up in special bandages. In other words – made into a mummy."

"Gross!" said Bo.

The professor shrugged. "It's just the way Egyptians did things. To them it was *dead* important!" He threw open the Time Shed's door. "Now come on – if I don't start exploring soon I'm going to explode!"

Pat and Bo followed him out into the cold, dark tomb of Tutankhamen. Professor McMoo lit a lamp. The golden flicker of flame showed the room was full of jewels and statues, comfy sofas and finely made pots and vases.

"Wow," said Pat, his voice echoing eerily. "Why did he need so much stuff down here if he was dead?"

"The Egyptians didn't think life stopped when you died," Professor McMoo explained. "To them it was more like moving house. You see, Pat, important dead people were buried with riches and servants in case they needed

them in the afterlife and—"

"Look!" Bo interrupted, pointing into the shadows.

Pat looked round. In the corner of the room there stood a very large case. It was covered in gold and gemstones, and shaped to look a bit like a human body.

"I'll bet Tooting Car Horn is in there!" Bo said, trotting towards it.

"Be careful, Bo," McMoo warned her.

"Oh, come on, what's it going to do to me?" she protested.

"He's more worried about what *you* are going to do to *it*!" said Pat.

But suddenly, as Bo approached, the front of the case wobbled. Then it started to topple forward . . .

25

"Hey!" Bo backed away. "Professor, we're under attack!"

"Get behind me," said McMoo bravely as the front of the case hit the ground with a deafening crash. To reveal . . .

. . . There was nothing inside at all!

The professor stepped forward to investigate. "The vibrations of our hoofsteps on the floor must have made the lid of the mummy case tip over."

"But where's the mummy?" asked Bo.

"I *want* my mummy!" joked Pat shakily. "This place is scary!"

"It's certainly very strange," said McMoo, holding up the lamp and looking about. "The mummy was here in 1922 when the tomb was rediscovered. So where's it gone?"

"Ugh," Little Bo groaned. "Look what I just stepped in."

Professor McMoo held up the lamp, and he and Pat peered to see.

A fresh cowpat lay on the floor, gently steaming.

"Was that you, Pat?" said Bo sternly. "I know you were scared, but—"

"I went in the field before we left!" Pat protested.

"Then perhaps the ter-moo-nator made this," said McMoo. He produced some tweezers and started to poke about in the muck. Then he jumped up in triumph. "Yes, just as I thought – iron filings!" He thrust the tweezers in Pat's face. "Look!"

Pat turned up his nose. "I'll take your word for it, Professor."

"So the ter-moo-nator has been here recently," Bo realized.

"And he might not be alone," said Professor McMoo. "Yak said there were other F.B.I. agents about, remember?"

Suddenly a muffled, terrifying groan rang out around the tomb.

"What was that?" whispered Pat fearfully.

Bo gulped. "I don't know. Didn't sound like a ter-moo-nator."

Then they heard the *CLOMP* . . . *CLOMP* . . . of heavy footsteps on the stone floor. Getting louder. Closer. Thumping towards them in the thick darkness.

"Whatever it is," said Professor McMoo gravely, "it looks like we're going to find out!"

Chapter Three

THE MUMMY, THE MOON AND THE MEDJAY

Suddenly, a large, lumbering shape came stamping out of the shadows. It was wrapped in dirty bandages, the loose ends trailing behind it like streamers. The glint of gold showed on its face. Dark eyes burned into the cows' own as the bandaged monster lifted a huge urn above its head and got ready to throw it.

"Aha!" cried Professor McMoo. "*There's* the mummy!"

"Duck!" Pat shouted.

"No, it's definitely a mummy," said McMoo.

"*Mooo*-ve!"

Little Bo shoved them both out of the way as the mummy threw the urn. It smashed into pieces right where they had been standing.

"That thing's alive!" Bo said as the mummy started to stalk towards them. "Thought you said Tooting-thingummy was dead?"

"Dead *scary*," said Pat. "RUN!"

"This way," McMoo exclaimed, bundling them ahead of him. The mummy bellowed and snorted with rage, and started to run after them.

They charged out through a large door and into the next pitch-black chamber. Pat felt his heart racing.

The light of the lamp was flickering and it was hard to see which way to go.

"Why are we running?" asked Bo. "I'll soon sort that mummy-dummy out. He'll *need* bandages by the time I'm through with him."

McMoo skidded to a stop at a shadowy crossroads. "We're running, Bo," he panted, "because whatever is going on here, Tutankhamen's mummy is a priceless piece of history. You can't just beat it up!"

Another bellowing roar echoed eerily from behind them, and Pat quivered. "Sounds like he agrees!"

"Quick, down here," said McMoo, charging off along the passage to their left. Pat and Bo ran after him. The clatter of their hooves on the stone sounded like machine-gun fire. Sinister shadows shook and danced along the stone walls and ceiling in the flickering light of the lamp. And still the monstrous, heavy footsteps pounded after them.

"But if we can't fight that thing, what *are* we going to do?" Bo demanded.

"Use our eyes instead of our fists," said McMoo. "And watch what it does."

"It chases us!" Pat gasped. "What more do we need to know?"

The stone tunnel wound round to the right. McMoo ducked inside a dark doorway on the left. "I wonder where this leads," he said.

WHAMMMM!

The professor crashed into something so hard it nearly knocked his nose inside out! Bo bashed into the back of him, and Pat bundled into the back of her. All three of them ended up in a squashed heap.

Pat struggled up, panting for breath. "What happened?"

"I think we ran into a wall," Bo told him. "The passage is a dead end!"

"Oh, my head," groaned McMoo.

"I'm seeing stars!"

"Are you badly hurt, Professor?" Pat asked anxiously.

"No, I mean I'm *really* seeing stars. Look." McMoo pointed up to a large square gap in the wall above them. "I must have whacked into the wall so hard it knocked out a loose brick."

Bo jumped up. "Where's that mummy? Is it coming after us?"

They listened. But the tomb was as quiet as . . . a tomb.

A wave of relief washed over Pat. "We must have given the mummy the slip!"

"But how come it's running about in the first place?" asked Bo. "And what happened to the ter-moo-nator who left that smelly present behind on the floor?"

"Perhaps the mummy scared him too," McMoo suggested, rubbing his sore nose. "A ter-moo-nator would certainly have the strength to charge his way out and block the hole behind him." He scrambled up to the hole in the wall. "Shall we see what's on the other side?"

"Go for it, Prof!" said Bo eagerly.

McMoo poked his head out through the gap. It was night-time in the Valley of the Kings. The big, full moon and twinkling stars shone down on an eerie stretch of cliffs and sand dunes and enormous statues. Impressive entrances had been carved into sides of the sandy mountains, to mark the tombs of other great pharaohs.

"Coast is clear," McMoo hissed back, and jumped down for a soft, sandy landing. Pat and Bo plopped down beside him.

But then suddenly ten big, burly men in skimpy red uniforms came into sight from behind a sand dune!

Bo glared at the professor. "Doesn't look a very clear coast to me!"

"Oh dear," said McMoo. "I recognize those uniforms. Bo, Pat, meet the Medjay – the Egyptian police. They keep law and order."

"And very big swords by their sides!" Pat noted nervously.

"Well, well," said the Medjay chief. "Looks like we've found some tomb robbers, trying to sneak out the back of Tutankhamen's place!"

"That's not true," said Bo fiercely.

But the chief ignored her. "The penalty is death!"

The Medjay drew their scary swords and closed in on the cows . . .

Bo put up her hooves in a kung-moo pose, and Pat lowered his head, ready to charge. But Professor McMoo just stood there, looking at his wristwatch.

"Don't mind me," he said. "Just checking the time."

"It's *time* for a quick getaway, Professor," Pat hissed. "What are you up to?"

McMoo just smiled. "Drop those swords," he told the Medjay chief firmly. "We are not robbers. We are cows— er, *people* – from a far-off land, and we have great powers."

The chief sneered. "Prove it!"

Pat held his breath. What was Professor McMoo going to do?

"Very well," said McMoo calmly. "I shall make the moon vanish from the sky."

"As if!" scoffed the chief.

But McMoo just smiled and pointed to the sky – and a gasp went up from the Medjay. The chief's jaw dropped so far he almost got a mouthful of sand.

Because the moon *was* disappearing! It was as if a great dark red shadow was sweeping over it.

Bo gulped. "How are you doing that, Professor?"

"I'm not," he murmured. "I simply remembered the date – about three o'clock in the morning on September 3rd, 1250 BC. I told you in the Time Shed we would find quite a sight outside, and this is what I meant – *an eclipse of the moon*!"

Pat gazed awestruck at the professor. "But how did you know there would be one now?"

McMoo grinned. "I enjoy reading old astronomical charts when I'm having my breakfast."

"If this magician can make the moon

disappear, what will he do to us?" wailed a frantic Medjay.

"Don't make us disappear," the chief pleaded. He and his men threw down their swords. "Please!"

"Oh, all right then," said Professor McMoo — just as the eclipse began to end. "Tell you what, I'll even bring the moon back."

The Medjay chief fell to his knees. "Such powers can only be granted by the gods. Which of them sent you, strangers?"

"Er . . . Ra, the sun god," McMoo pretended. "You can tell by our sunny natures."

"And if you don't believe us, we'll knock your heads together!" Bo added.

Pat sighed. "Ask the Medjay if they have seen the ter-moo-nator, Professor," he hissed. "Or a mad mummy on the loose!"

McMoo nodded. "Tell me, Chief – have you seen any big grey bulls coming out of this tomb recently?"

"We have seen no bulls anywhere, Great Professor," said the chief. "Nor are we likely to."

"What are you on about?" said Bo.

"It is very mysterious," said the chief. "Every last cow, bull and calf has disappeared from this land. Not a single one remains!"

Chapter Four

ENTER . . . THE MOO-MY!

"No cattle in the whole country?" Pat frowned. "What's happened to them all?"

"It began two months ago," the chief explained. "Cows went missing in the night. Calves cleared off. Bulls disappeared."

"Freaky," said Bo.

"I bet it's got something to do with the F.B.I.," said Pat in a low voice. "But what? Why?"

McMoo nodded. "Not forgetting How, When and Where?"

Bo couldn't hear them. "What?"

"We've already had that one," said Pat.

"What?" Bo frowned. "When?"

Pat groaned. "Shut up!"

"Why?" Bo demanded.

"OK, that's enough of that," said McMoo firmly.

"Enough of what, Great Professor?" asked the chief.

"Yes, *more* than enough!" he agreed. "Don't you start. Instead, please tell me – have you heard any strange noises coming from the tomb of Tutankhamen? Any groaning mummies running about?"

"Of course not, Great Professor," said the chief, bowing down so low his hair tickled McMoo's hooves. "Now, please, Great Professor and those who serve you. We must take you to the palace. Pharaoh Ramses will want to meet you."

"Goodness moo – Ramses the Great!" said McMoo excitedly. He turned to Pat and Bo. "He ruled Egypt for sixty-six years, you know."

Bo yawned. "Shouldn't we be doing more to stop the F.B.I. than meeting some old king?"

" 'Some old king'?!" echoed the professor, with a face like he'd sat on a nettle. But before he could give her a lecture on Ramses' importance, there was a loud shout from somewhere far away.

"OI! GET TO THE ENTRANCE OF TUTANKHAMEN'S TOMB, EVERYONE! NOOOOOOOOW!"

Pat froze. "Uh-oh," he said. "I recognize that voice."

"I don't believe it!" Little Bo cried. "It sounds like . . . Bessie Barmer!"

Professor McMoo groaned. "It must be that ancestor she talked about!"

"COME ON, THEN!" the wailing went on. "THE GODS HAVE TOLD ME – SHEBA UM-BARMER – TO GET EVERYONE DOWN HERE AT DAWN. SO DO AS I SAY OR YOU'RE FOR IT!"

"What is she on about?" Bo frowned.

"We'll soon find out," said McMoo, checking his watch again. "Dawn isn't far away."

"She's making enough noise to wake the pharaoh himself," said the chief. "Come, Great Professor. We shall shut this loopy woman up."

"Sounds good to me!" McMoo smiled at Pat and Bo. "And then we'll meet and greet the pharaoh. If we can get him on our side it will make our mission much easier."

It was a long trudge round to the other side of the cliffs to where the entrance to the tomb stood – and it took even longer because the Medjay kept insisting on smoothing out the sand in front of McMoo so his holy hooves didn't sink into it.

By the time they got near, the sun was starting to rise over the valley. In the thin dawn light, Pat saw that hundreds of people had gathered round – all on the say-so of the very large, very ugly woman who was standing on a huge block of sandstone in front of the tomb. Her hair was black and she was wearing a big white tent instead of mucky dungarees – but otherwise, Sheba Um-Barmer and Bessie Barmer looked exactly the same: totally disgusting!

"ROLL UP, ROLL UP," Sheba bawled like a circus ringmaster. "IT'S A TOMB

WITH A VIEW! YOU WILL NOT BELIEVE YOUR EYES . . ."

And then, McMoo couldn't believe *his* eyes as the crowds parted for an impressive figure in a big white hat, carried in a portable throne by four sweaty men.

"Who's that bloke in the silly headgear, Professor?" asked Bo.

"That's Pharaoh Ramses," said Professor McMoo, looking as happy as a calf with a cart full of clover. "To think I'm actually seeing him with my own eyes!"

46

Ramses stood up in his chair. "Who dares disturb the pharaoh?" he yelled.

Sheba Um-Barmer looked uncomfortable. "Sorry, Great King," she said, more quietly. "But the gods came to me last night! They appeared in a cloud of black smoke, and told me to bring as many people here as I could. How could I refuse? I am only a poor embalmer – I just stuff dead things for a living." She gave the pharaoh a wonky curtsey. "Is there anything *you* would like stuffed, Your Worship?"

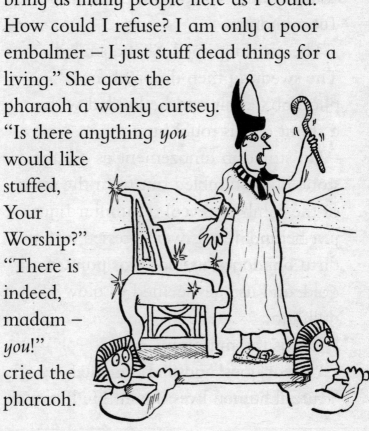

"There is indeed, madam – *you!*" cried the pharaoh.

He turned to the Medjay chief. "Deal with this disturbance, please."

"At once, Your Majesty," said the chief. He clapped his hands. "Everyone go home! Move along, there is nothing to see here—"

"*OH, YES THERE IS!*" came a commanding voice from the tomb of Tutankhamen.

The crowd gasped. Sheba smiled. The sweating men dropped the pharaoh's chair and he landed with a shout on his royal bum.

Pat stared in amazement as a huge stone block tumbled out from the front of the tomb to reveal a familiar figure just behind. Jewels were pressed into its dirty bandages, its face was painted gold, and its eyes seemed to glow with a dull light.

It was the mummy!

"Great gods!" gasped the chief. "Tutankhamen lives again! He has risen

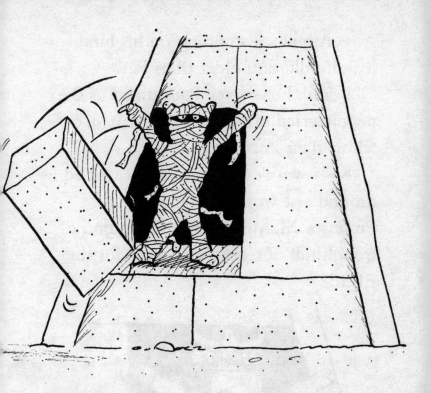

from his tomb!"

"He looks a bit of a funny shape," Bo
observed. "I didn't notice in the dark."

"Nor did I," the professor admitted.
"But it's a very *familiar* shape . . ."

Suddenly, the burly figure started
pulling off its bandages in front of the
incredulous crowd. The wrappings fell
away to reveal . . .

. . . A bullock standing on his hind legs, hardly any older than Pat!

"I don't believe it," Pat gasped as the people cried out in awe, or fainted, or fell to their knees.

"So it wasn't a mummy that chased us around – it was a *moo*-my!" said Professor McMoo. "And I'll bet you a trough full of tea he's working for the F.B.I.!"

Chapter Five

A SHOP FULL OF SECRETS

Pat looked between his sister and Professor McMoo in dismay as the crowd roared their approval of the mysterious moo-my.

"The boy king has returned in the shape of a cow!" a man shouted.

"*This* must be why all our cattle disappeared," cried another. "No earthly cow can compare with his splendour."

"He's not all that great," said Bo, bristling. "In fact, I think he looked better with the bandages *on!*"

But Ramses' voice rose above them all. "Who are you, strange creature?"

The bullock mooed loudly. "Hear me,

my people!" he cried, ignoring poor Ramses. "Seventy years ago, *I* was your pharaoh. Now the gods have sent me back from the afterlife in the form of a cow, to rule over you again." He cast off the last of the bandages. "Once, you knew me as Tutankhamen. Now you shall know me as Tutankha-*moo-oooooo* – and follow me again!"

"Yayyyyy!" cried the crowd.

"The people understand what that bullock's saying, Professor," said Pat anxiously. "How come?"

"He must be using a special translator," said Professor McMoo.

"That explains how they can hear him," Bo agreed. "But why do they *believe* him? They must be bonkers!"

McMoo shook his head. "The Ancient Egyptians believed their gods could visit the Earth in the form of a bull," he explained. "So a king coming back as a bullock would actually make sense."

"No wonder the F.B.I. chose this time to break through," said Bo.

But Pat could see that one Egyptian was *not* convinced – the real pharaoh, Ramses. "Wait, my people," Ramses shouted, struggling to be heard over the noise of the cheering crowd. "*I* am your king – not some bullock in bandages!"

But the people ignored him, bowing down to the young bull. "Hail our new pharaoh!" a man cried.

"He's an *old* pharaoh," someone else pointed out.

"Hail our new old pharaoh!" came the cry. "Tutankha-*mooooooooo*!"

Pat felt sorry for Ramses, who looked like he was going to start crying. But then sour old Sheba burst out of the crowd and barged right past them, with a face like she'd just swallowed a cowpat.

"I did a lovely job on those bandages," she grumbled to herself.

"And he's just yanked them all off! Stupid bolshy bulls. What a waste!"

"Sounds like Sheba knows more than she's been letting on," McMoo observed. "You and Bo get after her and find out what."

"Right you are, Prof," said Bo. "Don't worry, I'll get the truth out of her. A left hook, a right jab and a super-squirt from my udder will have her talking in seconds!"

"Or lying knocked out in a puddle of milk," said Pat with a sigh. "What about you, Professor – what are *you* going to do?"

"It looks like poor old Ramses has become an ex-pharaoh," said McMoo, thoughtfully. "I'll bet he could use a nice cup of tea – and I know that *I* could! I'll take him back to his palace."

"We'll report back as soon as we can," Pat promised.

As Pat and Bo hurried after Sheba, the chief of the Medjay looked worriedly at Professor McMoo. "I *was* going to take you to the pharaoh – but now I'm not sure which one!"

"I want to see Ramses at once," said McMoo. "He is the real ruler around here."

But by the look of the crowd, still going wild for Tutankha-moo, the professor was about the only one who thought so . . .

Pat and Bo followed Sheba through the backstreets of Edfu, a nearby town, all the way to a shabby, run-down embalming shop.

Just outside, another woman called to her. "Oi! Sheba! Your Ron come home yet?"

"No, he hasn't!" Sheba complained. "My no-good husband's been missing for weeks now, the lazy so-and-so."

"Quick!" said Pat. "While she's busy gassing to her neighbour, let's sneak into her store!"

"We could smash the window," Bo suggested, "and swing in commando-style on ropes. It'll be awesome."

"Except that Egyptians didn't have glass windows, and we don't have any ropes," Pat reminded her.

"You always take the fun out of things," Bo complained. "How about we just kick the door down instead?"

But as they went round the back of the small, sandy shop, they found a door standing ajar – much to Bo's disgust. She barged inside, and Pat nervously followed her.

It was dusty and musty in the shop's back room. The place was littered with badly stuffed animals – crocodiles, baboons, even a big dung beetle. The crocodile was so full of stuffing it looked more like a big green sausage. But a rat beside it had been so under-stuffed it resembled a prune with a tail. Some of the animals were halfway to becoming mummies, clumsily wrapped in dirty bandages.

"A blind gibbon wearing boxing gloves would have done a better job," said Bo.

"But it wouldn't earn as much," said Pat, pulling out a box from beneath a grimy table. It was full of jewels, vases and little carved statues. "Look at this lot!"

Bo picked up one of the statues. "Hey,
I saw one just like this in Tooting Car
Horn's tomb. D'you think Sheba
sneaked inside and stole it?"

"Or perhaps she *earned* it," said Pat.
"Sheba did a good job getting all those
people to wait outside that tomb at dawn."

Bo nodded slowly. "Without an audience, Tutankha-moo's comeback would have fallen flatter than a pancake!"

"And you can bet it wasn't the gods who told her to gather those people together," Pat went on. "It was the F.B.I.!"

"Hey!" Bo sniffed the air. "Can you smell something a bit iffy?"

Pat nodded. "Seems to be coming from that cupboard . . ."

They advanced on an old cupboard in the corner of the room. Bo yanked open the door . . .

Inside was a mummy!

Bo almost launched into full-on karate-cow commando mode – but Pat stopped her just in time. "It's OK," he said. "It's a *real* mummy. A human one, at that." Jewels were glued all over the figure's bandaged body. Its face had been painted gold and a large stripy headdress placed around the head.

"Bit posh, isn't it?" Bo remarked.

"Holy haystacks," breathed Pat. "Bo, what if this is the *real* Tutankhamen? His mummy wasn't in its case, remember?"

Bo nodded. "But how come he's ended up in Sheba's cupboard?"

Before Pat could think of an answer, the back door opened – and Sheba Um-Barmer burst in.

"What's all this, then?" she shrieked, arming herself with a stuffed elephant's trunk. Then, like a human tank, she charged towards them . . .

Chapter Six

BIG TROUBLE

"What are you two doing in my shop?"
Sheba growled, thwacking the elephant's
trunk against her palm like a truncheon.

"Us *three*, you mean," said Bo fiercely,
standing protectively in front of Pat.
"Me, my little brother – and Tooting
Car Horn!"

Sheba stopped dead in her tracks, her
face darkening.

Pat smiled grimly. "Yes, and I bet
Pharaoh Ramses would be very
interested to know about this – because
if that's the *real* mummy, it means that
Tutankha-moo the moo-my is a big
fat fake!"

Sheba's eyes narrowed. "Think you're clever, don't you?"

"A bit," Pat confessed. "But our friend Professor McMoo is *really* clever. He'll soon sort you out – *and* your bull bosses!"

"We'll see about that," snarled Sheba. With that, she raised the elephant's trunk and bundled towards them.

Swiftly, Bo grabbed the overstuffed crocodile and threw it in Sheba's path. With a high-pitched *URRK!* Sheba tripped over it and hit the ground so hard that the whole room shook. Suddenly chunks of the stone ceiling started raining down around them.

"Let's get out of here," Pat cried, jumping over Sheba's bulky body and tumbling out through the doorway.

"Oh, Pat! I was just warming up," Bo complained. "Anyway, what about the mummy?"

But then half of the ceiling gave way

completely. With a moo of alarm, Bo scrambled out – just as the cupboard with the mummy inside was buried completely.

Pat gulped. "There's nothing we can do right now. We must get back to the professor and tell him what we've discovered – then come back with some digging tools."

"Hey," said Bo. "What happened to Sheba?"

Pat stared at the rubble. "She – she must have been squished in the cave-in!"

But suddenly Sheba burst up from the ground like a giant balloon, covered in white dust. "My shop!" She shook her enormous fist at Pat and Bo. "I'll get you for this – you *and* this professor friend of yours!"

"Come on – run!" cried Pat, and Bo reluctantly charged after him through the sandy streets.

Sheba waddled over to a stuffed trout

half-buried in the rubble. Hidden
beneath it was a magical device that let
you speak to someone far away – her
bosses called it a "mobile phone". "Oh
yes," she breathed. "I'll fix you lot good
and proper – just you wait!"

★

65

Professor McMoo, meanwhile, had retired to the palace of ex-Pharaoh Ramses where he was enjoying a cup of Egyptian liquorice tea. He had to make it himself, because all Ramses' servants and guards had gone off to work for Tutankha-moo instead.

Ramses himself was looking very miserable. "To think," he said with a sigh, "I have been replaced by a cow!"

"Cheer up!" said McMoo. "At least you get to keep your palace." Although that was only because Tutankha-moo had told the crowd that he would rule Egypt from the Great Pyramid at Giza, further up the River Nile.

"The Medjay chief said he saw you work great magic," said Ramses. "Will you use that magic to help me win back my throne and my people, Great Professor?"

"Just Professor," said McMoo. "And yes, of course I'll help you. Because that talking bull is *talking* bull – he's just an impostor up to no good. YOU are meant to rule Egypt, not him."

Then suddenly there was a commotion at the palace doors – shouting and banging and breathless moos.

"Sounds like Pat and Bo," said McMoo, jumping up. "Excuse me, Pharaoh!" He dashed to the door. As he opened it, his friends fell inside, puffed out and sweaty.

"Sheba Um-Barmer has got Tutankhamen's mummy in her cupboard," panted Pat.

"*What?*" McMoo spluttered.

"She's keeping it hidden," Bo went on. "'Cause if pharaoh-face here went inside that open tomb and found the real mummy, he could prove the moo-my was an impostor."

"Hey, *I* told you that!" Pat protested.

"So Sheba is working for the F.B.I.,"

mused McMoo. "Of course! She's an embalmer, she makes mummies. And they needed someone to wrap up their moo-my in the proper style so everyone would believe he was the real Tutankhamen – transformed into a cow."

Pharaoh Ramses swept into the entrance hall. "What is happening, Great Professor?"

"My friends think they have found the real mummy of Tutankhamen," McMoo explained. "I'm going to go with them to find it and bring it back here."

"We might need a shovel or two," said Pat, his cheeks going red. "I'm afraid that Sheba's house sort of . . . fell over!"

"What?" McMoo looked accusingly at Bo. "All that's left of the real Tutankhamen — a priceless piece of history — and you've *buried* it?"

Bo grinned. "What are you going to do — tell *mummy*?"

"Think he probably already knows!" said Pat. "Now come on, we must hurry—"

"Not so fast," came the angry voice of the Medjay chief as he stormed inside with four men. "We have had a complaint from a Mrs Um-Barmer in Edfu. She says you two hooligans made her house collapse."

"Only a little bit!" Bo protested.

But the chief ignored her. "You are under arrest."

"Chief, have you gone bonkers?" cried Pharaoh Ramses. "The Great Professor here is a mighty magician with incredible powers!"

"Ah, yes! I'm coming to him," said the

chief with a nasty smile. "You might be interested to know, I've spent all morning in a chariot with mighty King Tutankha-moo."

"Your private life is none of my business," said McMoo politely.

The chief scowled. "Me and the boys were taking him to his new home in the Great Pyramid at Giza. We told him about you on the way. And do you know what he told us?"

"What a clever, dashing, sophisticated person I was?" said McMoo hopefully.

"No. He said you were a trickster and a tomb robber – just as I thought in the first place," said the chief. "He said the moon only vanished 'cause of something called an 'eclipse'. And he ordered me to arrest all three of you – and then throw you to the hungriest crocodiles I can find." The chief drew his sword and smiled nastily. "Come with me to meet your doom – and make it *snappy*!"

Chapter Seven

IN DE NILE

"Crocodiles?" Pat felt his knees start to knock as the four burly Medjay guards surrounded them.

"Couldn't you throw us to some nice hungry hamsters instead?" said the professor, with a winning smile.

"Bring on the crocs," Bo jeered. "I'll turn them into handbags before they can take a bite!"

"We shall see," said the chief. "Now move!"

"Listen, matey," boomed Ramses, making the four Medjay guards jump. "*I'm* the king round here and if anyone is throwing these tomb

71

robbers to the crocodiles, it's *me*!"

"Pharaoh Ramses, how could you?" cried McMoo, looking hurt. "We're trying to help!" But his words fell on deaf ears.

"You are not the king any more, Ramses," said the chief. "Tutankha-moo is our ruler now. And I'm afraid he wants me to confiscate all your belongings and take them to Giza."

"Ha," Bo snorted. "Still, never mind, eh? The decorations here are a pile of pants — you won't miss them!"

Ramses looked like he was about to explode, but then seemed to recover himself. "Of course, I shall give all I have to Tutankha-moo. I want to help him all I can." He smiled. "For instance, I know of a perfect spot to find *very* hungry crocodiles, not far from here."

"Really?" The chief smiled. "Very well. Take us there straight away."

The three C.I.A. agents were marched

out at swordpoint. McMoo sighed. "Sorry about this, you two," he said. "It seems I was wrong about Pharaoh Ramses being a great leader."

"A great twerp, more like," said Pat.

"Don't worry, Pat," said Bo. "Or you, Professor. I'll look after you."

"Thanks, Bo." McMoo smiled kindly. "I'm sure you will."

Pharaoh Ramses led them through his large, well-kept gardens and down to a grand little dock at the edge of a fast-flowing river.

"Ooooh, look — it's the Nile!" cried the professor. "Longest river in the world. Imagine that! It stretches on for over four thousand miles, goes through nine different countries—"

"And it's stuffed full of crocodiles," said Pat miserably, pointing to a cluster of ugly green reptiles lurking by the riverbank. Each was as long as a sofa, with giant twitching jaws.

"Oh. Oh dear." McMoo sighed. "I'm afraid a painful, hideous death is on the cards for us."

"I usually like playing cards," said Pat. He shuddered. "Everything except SNAP!"

"Never mind the crocs. Look at that cool big ship," said Bo, pointing to a very long, very grand boat that was moored to the dock by a thick rope. Its deckhouse was decorated blue and red and it had a gigantic billowing sail. "It's well posh. Whose is it, then?"

"That is my royal racing yacht," Pharaoh Ramses informed her.

"Not any more," said the chief. "As of now, it's Tutankha-moo's."

"Well in that case, someone had better take it to him, hadn't they?" said the pharaoh. And suddenly he shoved the chief with all his strength – down the bank and – *SPLOOSH!* – into the water.

"Aaagh!" cried the chief as the

crocodiles swam hungrily over. "Help!"
The Medjay guards abandoned their
prisoners and jumped into the water to
save him.

Pharaoh Ramses winked at Professor McMoo. "I was only pretending to go along with the chief," he explained. "Now, you can take my yacht and escape!"

"Cheers, Rammy-baby!" said Bo, blowing him a kiss. "You are a fair pharaoh after all!" She charged up the gangplank after Pat and McMoo. Once they were all on board the yacht, Pat chomped through the mooring ropes.

"Don't worry, Ramses," McMoo called as he steered the yacht away. "We will travel south to Edfu, dig out Tutankhamen's mummy, and bring it back here so you can prove to your kingdom that that cheeky bullock is an impostor!"

"Um, Professor? We *can't* go south," said Bo, pointing behind him. "Look!"

Pat gasped. "There's a Medjay ship coming straight for us!"

A long, narrow craft was approaching, rowed by fierce-looking guards.

"There's no escape," the chief shouted as he struggled out of the water. "You see, I ordered more troops to come here by boat – I *knew* you'd give us trouble."

"That baby crocodile behind you will give you more than just trouble," called McMoo.

The chief scoffed. "You expect me to fall for that old one?" But a moment later, he came streaking out of the water with a small green croc attached to his bottom.

"YEEOOOWW!" His guards flapped about trying to pull it off.

Ramses waved to McMoo. "Row north, my friends. Perhaps you will be able to double back later."

"What about you?" Pat called. "You'll be in trouble now too."

"I will lock myself in the royal toilet till you get back," Ramses told them. "It's solid gold, and I've got a good crossword to pass the time. Good luck!"

"I think we'll need it," said Bo. "That Medjay ship is almost alongside us!"

"Pick up an oar," Pat urged her.

"Good idea," said Bo. She picked one up – and then lobbed it at the Medjay ship, knocking two guards into the water. "Direct hit!" she cried.

"That wasn't quite what I meant," said Pat, slapping a hoof against his forehead. "How are we going to row now?"

"There's only one thing for it," said Professor McMoo. "Bo – you'll have to use udder-power!"

"Woo-hoo!" yelled Bo, running to the back of the yacht. "I'll give it a go, Professor!"

Pat stared as she hung over the side and dipped her lower half in the water. "What's she up to?"

McMoo grinned. "She's about to invent the outboard motor three thousand years early!"

The Medjay boat had almost caught up with them. Some of the men were standing up and waving their swords.

"Stand by for squirt-off," Bo called. Then she squeezed her udder as hard as she could. A huge stream of milk jetted into the water – and started to propel them downstream.

"Yee-haaa!" cried Pat as the yacht picked up speed.

Startled fishermen stared from the riverbanks. Cargo-boat captains gasped in disbelief. Bo's teats were like jets firing milk instead of flame, pushing the yacht along like a rocket. Soon the menacing Medjay ship had been left far, far behind.

Bo grinned at McMoo and her brother. "Lucky I missed being milked this morning, eh?"

"Too right," said Pat. "At this rate we'll be halfway to Giza in a couple of hours!" A worrying thought struck him. "Which means we'll be slap bang in the middle of Tutankha-moo territory."

"And how will we ever get back to find the mummy?" asked Bo.

"I don't know," said McMoo gravely. "But do you notice something?"

Pat shook his head. "What?"

The professor waved his hoof about. "There's so much lush grazing land here beside the river – but no cattle to graze on it!"

"Of course," said Pat, a shiver tingling down his long backbone. "I remember now – the chief said that every single cow had disappeared, didn't he?"

Bo nodded. "But where to?"

McMoo sighed crossly. "If only we knew what the F.B.I. is planning!"

The river started to grow busier the further north they went. Little two-man boats, big trading ships, tiny rafts made from bundles of reeds, they all floated down-river in the bright sunshine. Pat and McMoo steered the royal yacht in and out of the Nile traffic but soon the river was just too clogged to keep going.

"OK, Bo, stop the engine!" McMoo shouted.

"Thank goodness for that." Bo heaved her body out of the water. "I was getting cramp in my udder." She came dripping over to where McMoo and Pat stood at the side of the barge, staring out at the traffic. "Hey!" she yelled to a man in the nearest boat. "Where's everyone going?"

"Great Tutankha-moo has a gift for us," said the man excitedly. "It is a special drink he has brought from the gods – mu-mu juice!"

"His messengers are spreading word throughout the kingdom," said a man on a raft behind them. "Everyone must come to the palace and drink the mu-mu juice in the morning. He says it will change our lives for ever!"

"But change them *how*?" McMoo wondered. "Mu-mu juice? I don't like the sound of this one bit."

"*I* don't like being stuck in a watery traffic jam," Bo complained. "We're sitting ducks."

"Did they actually have ducks in Egypt?" wondered Pat.

"They do now," McMoo yelled, pointing behind him. "DUCK!"

Pat hit the deck and yelped as a spear

went flying over his head. He looked up to find Medjay guards were swarming over the riverbank.

"Tutankha-moo was right!" one guard shouted. "He *knew* his enemies would be travelling on the royal yacht."

"It is magic," cried another.

"More likely a communicator," said the professor, grimly. "The ter-moo-nator must have been watching the palace – he saw us escape, called up

Tutankha-moo and told him we were on our way."

"That rotten grass!" snarled Bo. Then her face softened. "Actually I could just do with a bit of grass right now."

"Hey!" shouted one of the Medjay.

"Yes, hay would be nice too," Bo agreed – then ducked again as a spear sailed over her head.

"Come on, men," said the Medjay leader. "These fools are trapped in the water with nowhere to run. Let's wade in and catch them . . ."

"What do we do now?" wailed Pat. "He's right – we're trapped!"

Chapter Eight

ESCAPE INTO DANGER

McMoo, Pat and Bo squashed themselves flat against the deck of the royal yacht while the Medjay waded ever closer.

"I've got an idea for a distraction," whispered Pat. "I could jump overboard, duck beneath the water, then pull off my ringblender to stop it working."

McMoo considered this. "The Medjay would see a boy jump in and a bullock come out." He smiled. "They would never dream it was the same person."

"And while they try to fish a 'boy' out of the Nile, the professor and I sneak away . . ." Bo whistled. "That's clever,

Pat. But you should let me do it."

"No. You're a better fighter than me," Pat reminded her. "You stay here and protect the professor. I'll see if I can sneak back and find that mummy."

"While you're gone, Bo and I will try to find out more about this mu-mu juice and the missing cows," said McMoo. "Good luck!"

Pat smiled bravely and took a deep breath. "Catch me if you can, Medjays!" he yelled, and leaped up into the air. He cleared the side of the yacht and hit the Nile with a super-huge splash.

"Quick – *now*!" McMoo jumped up and grabbed Bo by the hoof.

"But there's nowhere to go!" she protested.

"We'll use the boats as stepping stones!" he cried.

While the Medjay furiously searched the river for the young man they believed Pat to be, McMoo and Bo jumped from the side of the barge.

They landed with a *WHUMP* in a small fishing boat. From there they hurled themselves into a nobleman's barge before bouncing off into a little old man's canoe. That nearly capsized, so they quickly hopped across onto a big old cargo ship carrying planks of wood.

"Stop them, someone!" called the Medjay leader.

Some burly bare-chested men rushed from the cabin of the cargo ship to get McMoo and Bo. Bo stopped one of them in his tracks with a kung-moo kick, but the other one swung a plank of wood at the professor. McMoo dodged aside so the plank broke in two on the floor – then butted the man so hard he went flying up into the ship's rigging.

"That bloke's got invisible horns!" cried the burly man, tangled up in the ropes.

"And a brain the size of a badger!" McMoo agreed cheerily. "How else could I dream up a plan like this?" He tossed half the broken plank to Little Bo. "Surf's up!" So saying, he leaped overboard and splashed down into the water with the other half. Using it like a bodyboard, he started splashing away with all four hooves. "Paddle for your life, Bo!"

Bo jumped in after him, and was soon steering a nimble path on her plank through the heavy river traffic, away from the furious Medjay. They kept going and only stopped for breath some way down-river. The kerfuffle hadn't reached this far down the Nile, and luckily people had stopped pointing at them.

"Phew," said Bo, with a worn-out smile. "We made it!"

"Let's hope that Pat did too." McMoo sighed. "Come on. Let's see if we can get a closer look at that Pyramid of Giza — and the geezer who's living there!"

Further south, Pat pulled off his wet clothes and scrambled up the opposite bank of the Nile. The Medjay were too busy searching for a human bad-boy to notice a bright-eyed bullock leave the river.

The ringblender was now tucked safely under Pat's tongue, so he was no longer in disguise. However, since all the cattle in Egypt had gone missing, he knew he would stand out like a luminous cowpat in the dark. He had to find cover — and fast.

Pat dashed through the lush farmland that lined the banks of the Nile. After a while he came to a low building where grain was being stored.

I'll just rest here for a few minutes, Pat

thought. But as he lay down, the warm sun and the smell of grain made him feel drowsy. Worn out by his adventures, Pat dropped off to sleep.

When he woke again, he almost exploded with shock.

A ter-moo-nator was standing in front of him!

"Hello, little bullock," it said, with a sly smile. "Are you lost?"

Pat gulped. Luckily the ter-moo-nator didn't recognize him as a C.I.A. agent. It seemed to think he was just an ordinary, Egyptian cow.

"Are you wondering where all the other cows have gone?" it went on, green eyes glowing.

As a matter of fact, I am! thought Pat. He nodded hopefully.

"Come with me." The big grey bull led him to a small shed on the other side of the field. "Life is going to change a lot for cows in the next few weeks. The humans shall work for *us*, not the other way around! But first you must join all the others . . ."

The shed was dusty and full of harvesting tools. The ter-moo-nator tugged on a sickle – and Pat gasped as part of the floor slid away to reveal a secret tunnel, stretching down into the depths of the earth.

"Don't be afraid," said the ter-moo-nator. "There are tunnels like these leading from key fields all across the kingdom. I'll tell you more along the way . . ."

Pat blinked in disbelief. Without even trying, it looked like he was about to discover what the F.B.I. was up to.

But would he ever see McMoo and Bo again to let them know?

Cautiously, he followed the ter-moo-nator down into the steep tunnel. Once inside, the entrance slid shut behind him, closing with a clang.

Pat knew there was no going back now . . .

Chapter Nine

A CHILLY WELCOME

Professor McMoo and Bo were spying on the Great Pyramid from the top of a sandy cliff. Tutankha-moo stood proudly on a special platform, surrounded by crowds of Egyptians.

"Tomorrow I will give you yummy mu-mu juice to drink, my people!" cried Tutankha-moo. "I shall even pour some in the Nile. Just a few drops will make the water taste sweeter than dew from heaven!"

"What do you think will be in that stuff, Professor?" asked Bo. "Poison? Germs? Um . . . dew from heaven with added sugar?"

"I wish I knew," said McMoo. "If only we could find out what's *really* going on." Then, suddenly, he clapped his hooves in delight. "Well, well, look down there, what perfect timing – it's Sheba Um-Barmer!"

"What's perfect about it?" Bo squinted and saw the giant, wobbling shape of Sheba, far below in the backstreets of Giza, looking sneaky and dragging a big sack. "What's she even doing all the way out here?"

"Let's find out!" cried McMoo, bounding off down the rocky path like a mad mountain goat with rubber hooves. Bo followed him all the way down to the bottom of the cliff. "I wonder which way she was headed."

The next second, McMoo had his answer – as Sheba shambled round the corner with her well-stuffed sack!

"Grab her, Bo!" McMoo ordered.

Bo somersaulted through the air with

a war cry of "*Mooooo!*" Before Sheba could even shout out she was lying squashed to the ground with an udder in her face.

"You again!" Sheba groaned.

McMoo rummaged through her sack. "Well, well, what have we here? Looks like the mummy of Tutankhamen!"

"It's not," Sheba protested. "It's a parrot I'm having stuffed."

McMoo pointed to the man-sized bundle. "Quite a big parrot."

"I, er, overstuffed the beak a bit," said Sheba lamely. Then she sighed. "Oh, all right then. It *is* the mummy of Tutankhamen. After you wrecked half my shop, I called up the ter-moo-nator and told him what happened. He knows you're here and trying to stop him."

"I know he knows," said McMoo.

"And he *knows* that you know he knows," said Sheba.

Bo looked at the professor. "Did you know he knew that you knew he knew?"

"No," McMoo admitted. "Tell me, Sheba – once the ter-moo-nator knew that my team and I were on the scene, what did he do?"

"He told me to bring the mummy to the Great Pyramid so that you wouldn't find it again." Tears welled up in her bulging eyes. "When he finds out I've failed, I'm for it. Oh, if only my husband, Ron, would come back from wherever he vanished to!"

Bo's face softened. "Do you really miss him?"

"Of course I do." Sheba blew her nose noisily on the sleeve of her dress. "Life isn't the same since I haven't been able to bully him all day and make his life a misery!"

But the professor wasn't listening. "So you're on your way to the Great Pyramid, eh? Tutankha-moo's base." He grinned at Sheba. "With your help, perhaps Bo and I can sneak inside."

"OK," said Sheba. "As long as we can take the mummy too."

Bo frowned. "You'll really help us?"

"Why not?" Sheba smirked. "If you go to that pyramid, you'll be going to your doom. And I'll be in the ter-moo-nator's good books – delivering not just the mummy but two of his biggest enemies!"

"We shall see," said the professor calmly. "Come on, Sheba. We'll stick to the backstreets . . ."

They made their way cautiously towards the Great Pyramid. The main entrance was crawling with Medjay warriors in their distinctive red loincloths.

Bo scowled. "How are we supposed to get in there?"

"There's a secret way in," Sheba revealed. "The ter-moo-nator told me to use it so I didn't attract attention. Those guards will be expecting me, but they'll jump on you before you're anywhere near!"

"Don't be so sure," said McMoo, opening the sack. "Bo, get inside this thing and try not to squish the mummy. I'll crawl in after you and Sheba can drag us all inside."

Sheba scowled. "Why should I?"

"Because if the guards *do* find us in here, they will find Tutankhamen's mummy too." McMoo smiled. "Bo and I will very kindly explain how you were hiding it in your cupboard so every one would believe that Tutankha-moo was the real deal. And when they realize he's a fake and that you've helped him to trick everybody, they might decide they want to stuff YOU."

Sheba grimaced. "Oh, all right. But don't forget, the ter-moo-nator is inside that pyramid – he can sort you out all by himself."

"Just get dragging the sack, walrus-features," said Bo rudely.

Puffing, panting and cursing under her breath, Sheba managed to drag the huge bundle of bodies over to the secret entrance in the pyramid wall. The guards nodded to her in greeting. She knocked twice on a large brick and it slid open to

allow them inside. No sooner had she
dragged the sack through the secret door
than it slammed shut.

"Brrr," said McMoo, shivering as he
quickly climbed out of the sack into
pitch blackness. "It's cold in here."

"It's *freezing*," Bo complained, scrambling out after him and grabbing hold of Sheba before she could run away.

"It's dark too," said Sheba. "I'll just turn on the light switch." Suddenly, lights snapped on all over the vast chamber.

"Professor," Bo gasped. "This pyramid is *electric*!"

"And full of food," McMoo realized, staring around. The chilly chamber was stuffed full of grass, hay, corn and fruits. Huge fans in the ceiling blew out cold air. "Someone's turned this part of the pyramid into a solar-powered deepfreeze for cow snack supplies. They must be planning on staying for quite a while."

Then Bo gasped. "It's not just a deepfreeze for food, Professor. It's for *cows* too. Look!"

She pointed to a big chamber next

door. It was full of blocks of ice, like a giant ice-cube tray. In every block of ice, there was a cow.

And there – standing frozen solid in the front row – was Pat!

Chapter Ten

UDDERLY HORRIBLE!

"Pat!" gasped Bo. She let go of Sheba and ran to see. "Little bruv, what's happened to you? Are you all right?"

"He's fine," McMoo promised her, following the cables and wires that snaked from the deepfreeze to a bank of controls. "Bo, this is amazing! Pat and all these other cows aren't just frozen solid. They have been put into suspended animation."

Bo blinked. "Put into suspenders and emotion?"

"*Suspended animation*," he repeated. It means they won't age a day, no matter how long they stay hidden in here.

Once they are defrosted they will wake up as fresh as the day they were frozen." McMoo glared at Sheba. "Why are your bull bosses doing this?"

Sheba shrugged. "I don't know. But as long as they keep paying me with goodies from Tutankhamen's tomb they can do what they like!"

Bo scowled at her. "Can you get Pat out of this, Professor?"

"Let's see." McMoo started pressing buttons with his hooves. There was a bleep, a bloop and a loud buzz. Then Pat's block of ice started dripping with water. "Done it!" he cried.

Bo pointed to the other blocks of ice, which were also starting to melt. "But it's not just Pat you're defrosting. It's all of them!"

"Ah," said McMoo. "Well, no one's perfect." Suddenly, red flashing lights and screaming sirens went off, echoing madly around the chamber. He blushed. "Oh dear. The controls must have been alarmed."

"*I'm* alarmed!" cried Bo, covering her ears. "Let's thaw out Pat and get out of here!"

"Stuff your brother," Sheba squawked. "And I *would* too, if I had my way. But there will be no escape for you now . . ." She lumbered over to block the secret doorway. "Hee hee, you will never get past *me*. I'm just too good!"

"Pride comes before a fall," the professor noted – just as Sheba slipped in a puddle of melting ice and crashed headfirst to the floor, knocking herself out. "But not very long before a fall," he added.

Sheba's fall sent shockwaves through the whole pyramid – enough to split Pat's block of ice wide open!

"Pat!" yelled Bo as he stood there stiffly like a bullock-flavoured ice pop. "Are you OK? How did you even get here?"

"Special underground tunnel," Pat said sleepily over the din of the siren. "F.B.I. built loads of them . . ." He yawned. "That's a loud alarm clock. Is it time to get up?"

"It's time to get *out*," said McMoo. He jammed his horns into the workings of the alarm and pulled out some wires. The siren spluttered into silence. "Done it!"

"Too late," said Bo. "Look!"

A big white bull had come into the chamber – an F.B.I. agent. He was carrying a huge gun. "Halt," he cried. "Do not move!"

"Yeah, like that's going to happen," said Bo. She grabbed a hefty chunk of Pat's giant ice cube and slid it across the stone floor towards the bull like a giant bowling ball. It knocked him flying.

"You've bowled him over, Bo!" said McMoo happily.

"Professor," gasped Pat, starting to recover. "Everyone in Egypt is in terrible danger! The ter-moo-nator told me that

all cows had to go to sleep for months –
and that when we woke up again, we
would rule over humans!"

"But how?" Bo wondered.

"That's what I must find out," said
McMoo, straightening up. "Bo, other
F.B.I. agents may come looking here.
Can you hold them off while I try to
find the F.B.I. control centre?"

Bo nodded. "Piece of cake. With a
cherry on top. And whipped
cream. And sprinkles,
and—"

"Thanks, Bo,"
he said hastily.
"In the
meantime, look
after Pat and
these other
poor cows
waking up from
suspended
animation. They

111

will be very confused and need someone to lead them. Oh, and take care of that mummy in the sack – remember, it's priceless!"

Bo nodded. McMoo grinned. Then he sprinted past Sheba and the fallen agent and into the chambers beyond.

It was cold, dark and eerie in the pyramid. The only light came from the occasional flickering torch fixed to the walls. He ran along a tunnel that seemed to go on for ever. Then he heard voices coming from the hall ahead, and the quiet hum of machines.

"The alarm's stopped now," a gruff voice was saying. "Must have been a false alarm. Get on with the experiment, Bob."

Carefully, quietly, Professor McMoo crept inside to see what was happening.

The large hall had been turned into a spooky laboratory – computers buzzed and whirred, potions bubbled in glass beakers and thick white smoke drifted out of test tubes. A towering ter-moo-nator looked on as bulls in white coats and surgical masks went about their work.

At the back of the huge hall was a sort of pen crammed with grumpy-looking humans. There was also a strange glass chamber in the middle of the room with a man inside. He was big, bald and fat, with a glum expression. In front of him were a table and an empty glass.

A bull in a plastic hazard suit was speaking into an electronic recorder. "This is Doctor Buffalo Bob of the F.B.I. reporting," he said. "Subject Ron Um-Barmer has now drunk three cups of mu-mu juice . . ."

So that's what happened to Sheba's husband! Moo thought. *Kidnapped along with those other poor souls, to take part in bizarre bull experiments!*

"The mu-mu juice will soon affect the subject's body," Buffalo Bob went on. "Watch closely, gentlebulls. Any moment now . . ."

Suddenly, Ron Um-Barmer's left hand swelled up like a glove full of water. His fingers shrank into themselves and turned bright pink.

McMoo gasped – the man didn't have a hand any more.

It had turned into an UDDER!

The professor looked more closely at the humans in the pen. Sure enough, they had grown udders too, in all sorts of weird places. "Incredible," he gasped.

"Isn't it just?" said a voice behind him.

McMoo whirled round — to find that Tutankha-moo had crept up behind him with two bull bodyguards.

"You have found your way into my lair," said the evil moo-my with a wicked smile. "But you will never get out again . . ."

In an instant, the professor was surrounded by big burly bulls. "Sorry," he told them. "I don't give autographs."

The ter-moo-nator strode up to him. "Subject identified as Professor Angus McMoo," it droned. "You are a spy."

"A *genius* spy at that," said McMoo, trying to act unbothered. "For instance — I reckon I've just worked out your entire plan."

"Oh, really?" sneered Tutankha-moo.

McMoo nodded. "If a human drinks three cups of mu-mu juice, hey presto! They grow udders. By bringing the whole population here and making them drink the stuff, you'll give them *all* udders."

The ter-moo-nator narrowed its glowing eyes. "That is only part of our plan."

"I haven't finished yet, tin horns!" snapped McMoo. "You also plan to pour mu-mu juice into the Nile, the longest river in the world. The people of nine countries depend on it for drinking water – it will take a while, but eventually *they* will all grow udders too!"

"Correct," said Tutankha-moo. "And while humans stand helpless in milky confusion, I shall awaken my army of cows from suspended animation and conquer all of Africa in a surprise attack." He laughed, and his bodyguards quickly joined in. "Then, instead of humans milking cows, cows shall milk humans! And we shall use that milk to feed an ever-growing army of warrior calves who will grow and take over the ancient world . . ."

"History will be changed for ever," breathed Professor McMoo. "The moomy's curse!"

"Curse?" Tutankha-moo snorted. "Cows shall worship me for setting them free."

"But they *won't* be free, will they?" McMoo cried. "They will be forced to do whatever you say. Once they've fought all the humans, they'll end up fighting among themselves. Within a hundred years, the whole world could be destroyed – and any chance of a happy future for cows in Luckyburger lost for ever."

"Forget the C.I.A. and those fools from the future," said the ter-moo-nator. "Why not join us, Professor? The F.B.I. could use a bull as smart as you."

"I'd sooner take a matador out for a romantic supper!" McMoo retorted.

"Ooooh, can I come?" asked one of the bull bodyguards. He blushed as Tutankha-moo gave him a withering glare.

The ter-moo-nator advanced on McMoo. "You know, Professor, cows are affected by mu-mu juice too – much, much faster than humans. If they drink even a few drops, they grow udders everywhere."

"Aha," said McMoo. "That's why you're keeping your battle-cattle in suspended animation – so they can't drink the water and get infected by accident."

The ter-moo-nator smiled. "I do believe that *you* look thirsty, Professor." It pointed to a red bucket inside the glass chamber. "How would you like to taste our mu-mu juice right now?"

McMoo shook his head fiercely. "You can lead a cow to water but you cannot make him drink."

The ter-moo-nator held up his weapon. "You can if you've got a big gun!"

"You metal-brained monster," hissed McMoo. He looked around desperately for an escape route, but there was none. The bull bodyguards were already herding him towards the glass chamber, where Ron still sat staring at his new udder.

"I wonder where your udders will grow, Professor," Tutankha-moo chortled. "I shall keep you in the glass room for ever, Professor, so my subjects can laugh at you. Ha ha ha!"

The other bulls in the room joined in the laughter.

"You're all udderly mad!" stormed McMoo.

"And soon *you* will be udderly all over," said Buffalo Bob, checking his hazard suit. "Udders here, udders there, udders EVERYWHERE!"

The mad bull scientist unlocked the door to the glass chamber . . .

Chapter Eleven

MOO-HEM AND MADNESS

"STOP!" came a commanding voice from the lab doorway. And much to Professor McMoo's relief, everyone *did* stop.

Then he saw why.

A tall, half-bandaged cow with a bright blue udder was walking into the room on her hind legs. She was covered in jewels that shone and glinted in the flickering firelight. A huge herd of ordinary cows, calves, bullocks and bulls followed close behind her, watching her with awe.

McMoo frowned. The jewels looked like those adorning Tutankhamen's mummy. And unless he was very much mistaken, the bandages were Tutankhamen's too.

The professor breathed a huge sigh of relief – it was Little Bo in disguise!

"Once, I was Queen Nefertiti," Bo said in a posh, quivering voice. "Now I have returned as Queen *Heffa-teaty*! I have come back from the afterlife to rule kindly over all cows. And I'm here to tell *you*, my lad – stop being such a naughty boy and go to your room!"

"What?" The regal bullock spluttered with rage. "How dare you tell me what to do?"

Bo crossed her arms. "Because as your army of cattle here all know – I'm not just any old moo-my. I'm your *moo-my-in-law*!"

Pat popped out from behind Bo. "She has a point, Tutankha-moo, don't you think?"

"She certainly *will* have a point!" said

Tutankha-moo, tossing his head crossly. "The point of my horns in her backside. Then she will really need those bandages!"

The crowd of cows gasped in horror. They were simple cows, and shocked that anyone could talk to their mummy-in-law in that way.

Pat turned to them. "Now you see your ruler as he truly is," he shouted. "A mean bully who uses force to get his own way!"

"Rebel bullock will remain silent!" grated the ter-moo-nator.

"Destroy him!" Tutankha-moo bellowed at his would-be army of cows. "You heard me. Squish him flat!"

"See what I mean?" said Pat triumphantly. Then he yelped as the ter-moo-nator started stomping towards him.

"Tutankha-moo must be stopped!" cried Bo. "He must be made to sit on the naughty-step pyramid until he can behave himself properly. Get him, cows! Heffa-teaty, your queen, commands it!"

All whipped up, the cows mooed ferociously and surged forward to get their ruler. Luckily, as they did so, they trampled the ter-moo-nator into the ground before he could reach Pat. With a snort of panic Tutankha-moo turned and ran.

Pandemonium broke out in the F.B.I. lab!

The bodyguards stared round in alarm, not sure what to do – and McMoo took his chance. He shoved them aside with all his strength and sent them crashing into Buffalo Bob. Bob, in turn, went crashing into his test tubes and beakers.

"Professor!" Pat shouted, rushing over. "Are you all right?"

McMoo ignored him, staring at Bo's bandages. "I simply cannot believe you *unwrapped* the priceless mummy of Tutankhamen!"

Bo's face fell. "Sorry, Professor."

"Sorry?" He hugged her. "It was a BRILLIANT idea. Heffa-teaty, indeed – that's fabulous!"

"Well, you did say those cows needed a leader," said Bo happily. "Pat helped dress me up and we led the cows here."

"Good plan," said McMoo.

But Pat was frowning. "Erm, that's what I thought at first. But now I think they're out of control!"

The Egyptian cows were running amok. All those weeks in suspended animation had left them energetic and over-excited. They chased Tutankha-moo around the room faster

and faster. Scientists scattered. Beakers
were broken. Notes were trampled.

"Help me," cried Tutankha-moo,

jumping up onto a lab bench beside the glass room, scattering potions and powders in all directions. "Somebody help me!"

And then the ter-moo-nator rose up stiffly from the floor, its green eyes blazing with anger. It strode over to the lab bench and aimed its enormous gun at the hyperactive herd. "Stop," it droned. "All running cows will be ter-moo-nated!"

"Don't think so, mate!" Thinking fast, Bo whipped off one of her bandages and turned it into a lasso.

With an expert flick of her hoof, she managed to hook it over the ter-moo-nator's huge horns. "Professor, Pat – help me!"

At once, Pat and McMoo saw what she was planning. They grabbed hold of the bandage with her – and pulled with all their strength.

The ter-moo-nator made a rude electronic noise as it was yanked off its feet and smashed into the lab bench. Tutankha-moo lost his balance and fell into the creature's robotic arms. The ter-moo-nator staggered back under his weight, smashed through the wall of the glass chamber and collapsed in a heap at Ron Um-Barmer's feet.

Ron grabbed his chance. "Time for a taste of your own mu-mu medicine!" he cried – and with his good hand, he emptied the big red bucket of mu-mu juice all over their heads!

The ter–moo–nator glubbed and
spluttered. Tutankha-moo wiped his lips
in a panic.

But it was too late.

Almost at once, an udder grew out
from the top of Tutankha-moo's head.
Another soon sprouted from his back,
and yet another dangled down from his
neck. "Help!" he cried. "Udder attack!"

The Egyptian cows stopped charging
about at last, transfixed by the strange
sight. The mu-mu juice was already

working on the ter-moo-nator too. The grey robo-bull snorted with rage as bright pink udders ballooned from his cheeks. Even the robotic panel on his side grew a small clockwork udder.

Ron Um-Barmer laughed and jeered at his former captors, and all the other kidnapped people joined in from their pen at the back of the chamber.

"A fitting fate for a fake pharaoh and his friend," McMoo declared. "Victims of their own wicked scheme!"

"Mission abort!" snarled the ter-moo-nator miserably, his unwanted udders wobbling like pink jellies. "Repeat, mission abort. F.B.I. Command, get us out of here!"

With a last flick of their unlikely udders, Tutankha-moo and the ter-moo-nator faded from sight in a haze of dark smoke. The dazed Buffalo Bob and his fellow scientists all vanished too. F.B.I. Command always recalled its agents if their plans were ruined.

For a few moments, Pat, Bo and Professor McMoo stood still in silence. The only sound was the mooing of the baffled Egyptian cows.

"We did it," said Bo slowly. "We really did it!"

Pat whooped. "We beat the F.B.I.!"

"Good work, you two." Professor McMoo beamed at his young friends. "Thanks to us, the moo-my's curse has been lifted – while the moo-my himself will be cursing all the way back to the twenty-sixth century!"

Chapter Twelve

THE FINAL SQUIRTS

There was no time for Professor McMoo and his friends to sit back and enjoy their victory. They had too much to do.

While McMoo worked on a potion that would reverse the effects of mu-mu juice, Pat and Bo rounded up all the confused Egyptian cows in the Great Pyramid. "I'm sorry you were kidnapped and told those stories about taking over the world," Pat told them. "But one day, all cows will enjoy a better paradise than the one Tutankha-moo promised you – a paradise built on kindness, not cruelty."

It was an impressive speech. But the cows were too busy mooing and eating the gigantic stockpile of grass and hay left in the pyramid to bother listening.

Someone else wasn't listening either. She never did. "Oooooh, my head!" groaned Sheba Um-Barmer. "What happened?"

"Sorry, Sheba," said Bo. "Your F.B.I. bosses have pushed off and left you with nothing."

'But we *have* found your husband," Pat added.

"WHERE IS HE?" Sheba bellowed, and steamed out of the chamber like a wobbling juggernaut to find him.

"Uh-oh," said Pat, and he and Bo raced ahead of her back to the lab. To their surprise, Mr Um-Barmer was standing beside McMoo outside the glass room.

McMoo grinned at his friends. "I've come up with the cure!" he informed them. "It won't take long to work. Then Mr Um-Barmer and the other people kidnapped for those F.B.I. experiments can go back home."

"RONNNNN?" came a thundering voice from outside the lab.

Pat gulped. "I'm not sure he will want to!"

"Where have you been?" Sheba demanded, marching up to her husband. "There's tons of housework for you to do, you still haven't put up those shelves and that garden doesn't irrigate itself, you know. And don't think having a dodgy hand will get you out of anything . . ."

Ron sighed as she went on and on, and turned to the professor. "If I'm cured, will my hand go back to normal?"

"Oh, yes," McMoo assured him.

"Pity," said Ron. "Reckon it could come in useful!" So saying, he squeezed

his fingers — and sent a squirt of milk
into Sheba's eye!
"See what I
mean?"

"Ugh!" Sheba scrunched up her face,
but it was so crumpled anyway you
could hardly tell the difference. "Leave
off!"

"Leave off yourself, woman," said
Ron, and gave her another squirt in the
face. Then he ran off quickly before she
could clobber him.

"I'll get you for this!" she promised,
thumping out of the chamber in pursuit.

"Whoa!" came a rough, familiar voice. "Think I'd sooner tackle a ter-moo-nator than face that woman on a dark night!"

Bo beamed. "It's Yak!"

"The director of the C.I.A. in person!" McMoo declared. "What are you doing here?"

Yak strutted inside. "When F.B.I. Command recalled their agents, we homed in on their time signal. It led us here in our time machines." He stared around. "Looks like you had quite a fight on your hands."

"You could say that!" Pat looked around the trashed lab. "There will be a lot of clearing up to do."

"We'll take care of it," Yak promised. "There won't be any trace left behind. This was a big victory for the C.I.A., troops. Well done, all of you!"

Pat grinned. "C.I.A.: eleven out of ten. F.B.I.: nil."

"Don't you mean *Nile*?" said McMoo. And he laughed as the sound of his friends' groans filled the echoing chamber.

Working together, the Cows in Action soon tied up all the loose ends.

Queen Heffa-teaty made her one and only public appearance on the steps of the Great Pyramid. "I've sent Tutankha-moo back to the gods for being a naughty boy," she told the gathered crowds. "He was making up that stuff about mu-mu juice – there's no such thing." She winked at Pat and the professor, standing beside her. "And now *I'm* off too. I command you all to follow Pharaoh Ramses, just as you did before."

Ramses pushed his way out of the crowd and climbed the steps of the pyramid, whooping for joy and kicking his heels in the air. "Thank you, young Bo," he said. "And you, Professor, and you too, Pat." Then he turned to face the enormous crowd. "Hello, everyone, it's good to be back. I would like to celebrate with an ENORMOUS feast for you all!"

The crowd went wild. Leaving the happy Egyptians to plan their super-supper, Bo slipped away with Pat and McMoo to the back of the pyramid. "Heffa-teaty's in retreat-y," she said, pulling off her grubby costume. "And good riddance! Those bandages were well itchy."

"Well, I doubt Tutankhamen will complain!" McMoo smiled. "We'll wrap him back up with his jewels, drop him off in his tomb, hop inside the Time Shed and be on our way!"

With everything safely taken care of, the three cows travelled back to their quiet, sleepy farm in the twenty-first century. The Time Shed landed in the exact same spot just a split-second after they'd left. To anyone watching, it seemed to have gone nowhere at all.

McMoo stuck the kettle on. "Time for a fresh cuppa to celebrate our return!" he said.

But someone didn't sound in the mood to celebrate. "Oi!" came a fierce shout from outside. "Where did you get to, you crummy cattle?"

Pat gasped. "It's Bessie Barmer!"

"After seeing Sheba, I'll almost be glad to deal with Bessie again," said Bo.

McMoo whipped off his glasses, hid the kettle under some straw and pulled on the big, bronze lever. The futuristic controls and computer screens folded back into the walls, floor and ceiling – just as Bessie barged in.

"Hmm," she said, looking at each of the cows in turn. "Well, at least in here you can't get up to any mischief . . ."

"Moo," said McMoo in agreement.

Bessie turned and stomped out of the shed. The moment the door closed, Pat, Bo and McMoo burst out laughing.

Bo plopped some tea bags in the teapot. "I wonder if we'll ever meet any more of her ancestors."

Pat smiled. "We'll find out soon enough."

"We certainly will." Professor McMoo grinned at his friends as he brewed up the tea. "The F.B.I.'s danger may be *past*, but we'll always be *present* to stop them in the *future* – whatever it takes!"

THE END

IT'S 'UDDER' MADNESS!

Genius cow Professor McMoo and his trusty sidekicks, Pat and Bo, are star agents of the C.I.A. – short for COWS IN ACTION! They travel through time, fighting evil bulls from the future and keeping history on the right track . . .

When Professor McMoo invents a brilliant TIME MACHINE, he and his friends are soon attacked by a terrifying TER-MOO-NATOR — a deadly robo-cow who wants to mess with the past and change the future! And that's only the start of an incredible ADVENTURE that takes McMoo, Pat and Bo from a cow paradise in the future to the SCARY dungeons of King Henry VIII . . .

It's time for action.

IT'S UDDER MOO-HEM!

Genius cow Professor McMoo and his trusty sidekicks, Pat and Bo, are star agents of the C.I.A. – short for COWS IN ACTION! They travel through time, fighting evil bulls from the future and keeping history on the right track ...

Professor McMoo and his fellow intrepid agents are travelling in their time machine again! This time they are off to the time of the Romans, where they will meet terrifying gladiators and a crazy emperor!

It's time for action.

Collect them all!

Riddle of the Raptors

The Hatching Horror

The Seas of Doom

The Mind-swap Menace

The Skies of Fear

The Space Ghosts

Day of the Dino-Droids

The Terror-Bird Trap

The Planet of Peril

Teeth of the T. rex

The Star Pirates

www.astrosaurs.com